the Fearsome Beastie

Giles Paley-Phillips

For Megan, Verity, Ben & Thomas

Illustrated by Gabriele Antonini

On a dark and snowy winter's night,
when folk switch off the bedroom light,
from far away, a ghastly noise,
wakes up sleeping girls and boys.

A fearsome beastie with sharp claws
has left its cave with dripping jaws.
The girls and boys start to quiver
the thought of beastie makes them shiver.

Over hills, through fields and streams,
below the moon that shines and gleams.
Beastie travels all the night,
arriving just before dawn's light.

The children hide beneath the stairs,
behind the drapes and under chairs.
"Sshhh" says one, "don't make a sound
if you do we will be found."

But it's too late, along the street
the beastie seeks a special treat.
It bares its claws, it cracks its tails,
its fangs look like old sharpened nails.

The children scream and make a fuss.
"The beastie wants to gobble us."
But beastie sits down in a heap,
begins to sob, then wail and weep.

"I only want us to play,
that's why I visit you today!"

On hearing this, the kids felt bad,
they didn't want to make him sad.
But beasties can be very sly
and as the children get close by...

His tears of sadness turn to roars,
then beastie gnashes dripping jaws.
One by one he eats them all
including Suzie, Clyde and Paul!

But doesn't notice little Pete
(the only one he doesn't eat)
run as quickly as he can
to find the house of his old Gran.

She owns a giant woodman's axe
(chopping wood helps her relax).
He tells old Gran what beastie did.
She says, "you are a clever kid."

They run as quickly as they can,
for dear old Gran has hatched a plan.
Still sitting there upon the street
is beastie wanting extra meat.

But Gran yells out "Just you stop"
then lifts the axe and with a chop,
she cuts the beastie right in two
and says "let's make a beastie stew!"

Before she puts him in the pot
(here comes the best bit of the plot)

All the little girls and boys,
holding their most favourite toys,
come running out of beastie's tummy,
each one crying for their mummy.

So if at night you hear a beast,
looking for a kiddie feast.
Just remember Pete's great plan,
to go and fetch his dear old Gran.
For beasties who play tricks on you,
will end up as a beastie stew!

GRRRRRRRRRRRRRRRRRRRrrrrr

'The Fearsome Beastie'
is an original concept by
author Giles Paley-Phillips

© Giles Paley-Phillips

Illustrated by Gabriele Antonini
Gabriele Antonini is represented
by Advocate Art Ltd
www.advocate-art.com

**PUBLISHED BY MAVERICK ARTS
PUBLISHING LTD**

©Maverick Arts Publishing Limited (2011)
Second Edition, October (2011)

Studio 4,
Hardham Mill Park,
Pulborough,
RH20 1LA
+44(0) 1798 875980

ISBN 978-1-84886-66-7

arts publishing

www.maverickbooks.co.uk